Red shoes dazzling — perched on a pedestal in the shop window as if on a throne.

"I want those, Nana," Malika says to her grandmother as they pass the shop.

"We'll see," Nana says with a wink. "Looks like you could use a new pair."

Surprise!
Red shoes nestled — in a shoebox under
tissue paper on the kitchen table!
Nana smiles her secret smile.

Malika laughs and slips them on quick, quick.

Red shoes walking,
click-clack-click — across the floor
on Malika's feet . . .

Swish, swish, swish around the living room . . .

Click-clack-clack — down the hall . . .

Then out the door and around the block Malika goes,
to show off her new red shoes.

Carefully, carefully on the first day of school
Malika walks in big galoshes that hide her shoes from the rain.
She wants to keep them dry when she jumps in puddles!

Red shoes dancing — on Daddy's feet
when they go to Auntie's wedding in the fall.

Jackson
Wedding

Red shoes kicking Cousin Jamal under the table at Nana's Christmas dinner as he tries to snitch Malika's buttery biscuit.

Red shoes stomping home when Malika and her best friend Keisha have a fight. Malika is mad and sticks to it.

Red shoes jumping double Dutch at Keisha's birthday party after they make up.

Then – oh no!
Red shoes pinching — when Malika squeezes them on
to wear to Nana's birthday dinner at a restaurant.

"My shoes are too small," Malika says sadly. And all through dinner her red shoes don't let her forget that her feet have grown!

65

Red shoes in the window at the resale shop where Nana and Malika have taken them to be resold so somebody else can enjoy them.

Softly, softly, Malika says goodbye to her wonderful red shoes.
They were her favorite shoes ever.

Inna Ziya spies the red shoes dazzling in the shop window. She knows just the little girl who will love them!

Now they are squeezed into her luggage bound for Africa!

Information 📍 ↑

Gates D6-D24 ✈ →

Airline Train 🚌 ←

Red shoes under Inna Ziya's
bench in the marketplace where
she sells her clay pots.

They are waiting for Amina,
the girl who fasted half the month
of Ramadan. The girl who deserves
a special gift.

And here she comes at last, holding her mother's hand.

Inna Ziya smiles down at Amina.
"I promised you a gift, and here it is."

Red shoes are passed to Amina's waiting hands.
"Thank you, Auntie," she says.
"They are *so* beautiful!"

Then later, red shoes riding on the *tro-tro* on Amina's lap.

Back at home, Amina's little sister, Halima, rushes to see the gift for the girl who fasted half the month of Ramadan, because someday she hopes to do the same.

Amina lets her try
them on, but just for a little while.

Halima will have them soon enough . . .
when Amina's feet grow too big
and Halima's feet grow big enough.

Now the red shoes are tucked safely under the bed, waiting to be worn on very special days.

Meanwhile, back on the other side of the ocean, Malika wonders: *Whatever happened to my beautiful red shoes. . . .*

. . . I wonder if someone is wearing them right now!

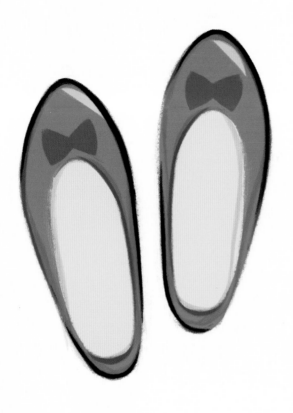

For Khadijah   –K.E.

For Gabby   –E.G.

Special thanks to Carina Ray, Associate Professor of African and African American Studies, Brandeis University, for her thoughtful reading and sensitive comments.

Library of Congress Cataloging-in-Publication Data available

ISBN 978-1-338-11460-7

10 9 8 7 6 5 4 3 2 1   20 21 22 23 24

Printed in China   38
First edition, September 2020

Ebony Glenn's illustrations were rendered digitally with Adobe Photoshop
using chalk, paper, and watercolor textures.
The text type was set in 16-pt. BernhardGothicSG Medium.
The display type was set in Miltonian Tattoo.
The book was printed on 128 gsm Golden Sun Matte and bound at RR Donnelley Asia.
Production was overseen by Catherine Weening.
Manufacturing was supervised by Shannon Rice.
The book was art directed and designed by Marijka Kostiw, and edited by Dianne Hess.